An Old-Fashioned THANKSGIVING

By Louisa May Alcott

Illustrated by Jody Wheeler

Ideals Children's Books • Nashville, Tennessee
an imprint of Hambleton-Hill Publishing, Inc.

Published by Ideals Children's Books
An imprint of Hambleton-Hill Publishing, Inc.
Nashville, Tennessee 37218

Printed and bound in Mexico

Library of Congress Cataloging-in-Publication Data

An Old-Fashioned Thanksgiving / adapted from the original by Louisa May
Alcott ; illustrated by Jody Wheeler.
p.   cm.
Summary: Follows the activities of seven children in nineteenth-century New
England as they prepare for the Thanksgiving holiday while Mother is away
caring for Grandmother.
ISBN 0-8249-8630-X (lib. bdg.)
ISBN 0-8249-8620-2 (trade)
ISBN 1-57102-053-5 (paper)
[1. Family life—Fiction. 2. Thanksgiving Day—Fiction. 3. New England—Fiction]
I. Wheeler, Jody, ill. II. Alcott, Louisa May, 1832–1888. Old-fashioned
Thanksgiving.
PZ7.0452   1993
[Fic]—dc20   93-20352
*   CIP*
*   AC*

The illustrations were rendered in watercolors.
The display type and text type were set in Cheltenham.
Color separations were made by Rayson Films, Inc.
Printed and bound by R.R. Donnelley & Sons.

Designed by Harvill Ross Studios Ltd.
Special thanks to Gail Niemann-Mayer

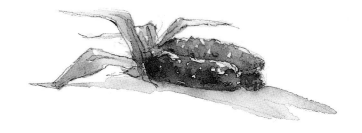

For the Wheeler sisters,
Margaret, Jane, and Betty
—J.W.

Many years ago, up among the New Hampshire hills, lived Farmer Bassett with his wife and a houseful of sturdy sons and daughters growing up about him. They were poor in money, but rich in land and love. Their wide acres of wood, corn, and pasture lands fed, warmed, and clothed the flock, while mutual patience, affection, and courage made the old farmhouse a very happy home.

November had come and the crops were in. Barn, buttery, and bin were overflowing with the harvest that rewarded the summer's hard work. In the fireplace a cheerful fire roared, and savory smells were in the air. Down among the red embers, saucepans simmered, suggestive of an approaching feast.

A white-headed baby lay in the cradle, now and then lifting his head to look out, sucking the rosy apple for which he had no teeth to bite. Two small boys sat on the wooden settle shelling corn for popping and sorting hazelnuts. Four young girls stood at the long table, busily chopping meat, pounding spice, and slicing apples. Farmer Bassett and Eph, the oldest boy, were doing chores outside, for Thanksgiving was at hand and all must be in order for that time-honored day. To and fro, from table to hearth, bustled buxom Mrs. Bassett, all flushed and floury.

"Only one more day and then it will be time to eat," said Seth to Sol, as he cracked a nut as easily as a squirrel.

"I'd like to have Thanksgiving every day," answered Solomon, gloating over the table filled with food.

"Not me," cried their mother, as she plunged her plump arms into the bread dough and began to knead.

"I think it's real fun to have Thanksgiving at home," said Tilly, the eldest daughter, pausing to take a sniff of her spicy pestle. "But I'm sorry that Gran'ma is sick, and we can't go there as usual."

"Here's a man comin' up the hill lively! Guess it's Gad Hopkins. Pa told him to bring a dezzen oranges if they warn't too high!" shouted Sol and Seth, running to the door, while the girls smacked their lips at the thought of this rare treat. Baby threw his apple overboard, as if getting ready for a new cargo.

But all were disappointed, for it was not Gad with the much-desired fruit. It was a stranger, who threw himself off his horse and hurried up to Mr. Bassett with some brief message that made the farmer drop his ax.

The man said old Mr. Chadwick told him to tell Mrs. Bassett her mother was failin' fast, and she'd better come today.

A few words told the story, and the children left their work to help their mother get ready. By the time the old yellow sleigh was at the door, Mrs. Bassett was waiting with the baby done up like a small bale of blankets.

"Now, Eph, you must look after the cattle and keep up the fires, for there's a storm brewin'," said Mr. Bassett.

"Tilly, put extry comfortables on the beds. I shall come back the minute I can leave Mother. Pa will come back tomorrer night, anyway, so keep snug and be good."

"Yes'm, yes'm—good-bye, good-bye!" called the children, as Mrs. Bassett was packed into the sleigh and driven away, leaving a stream of directions behind her.

Eph immediately put on his biggest boots and surveyed his responsibilities with a paternal air. Tilly tied on her mother's keys and began to order about the younger girls. They soon forgot Granny and found it great fun to keep house all alone.

The few flakes that caused their father to predict bad weather soon increased to a regular snowstorm, for up among the hills winter came early and lingered long. But Tilly got them a good dinner, and Eph kept up a glorious fire.

When the moon-faced clock behind the door struck nine, Tilly tucked up the children under the "extry comfortables" and, having kissed them all around as Mother did, she crept into her own nest.

When they woke, it was still snowing; but the little Bassetts jumped up and broke the ice in their pitchers. After a brisk scrub, they went downstairs with cheeks glowing like apples.

"Now about dinner," began Tilly.

"Ma didn't expect us to have a real Thanksgiving dinner," interrupted Prue, doubtfully.

"I can roast a turkey and make a pudding as well as anybody, I guess," cried Tilly, determined to enjoy her brief authority.

"Yes!" cried all the boys, "Let's have dinner—Ma won't care."

"Pa is coming tonight, so we won't have dinner till late. That will give us plenty of time," added Tilly.

"Did you ever roast a turkey?" asked Roxy with interest.

"Should you try?" said Rhody, in an awestruck tone.

"You will see what I can do. All you have to do is let me work," commanded Tilly.

So Tilly attacked the plum pudding. She had seen her mother do it many times, and it looked easy. But she forgot both sugar and salt, and she tied the preparation so tightly in the cloth that it had no room to swell, so it would come out as heavy as lead and as hard as a cannonball. Happily unconscious of these mistakes, Tilly popped it into a pot of boiling water.

"I can't remember what flavorin' Ma puts in," Tilly said, as she soaked her bread for the stuffing. "Seems to me it's sweet marjoram or summer savory, so let's put in both. The best herbs are in the attic—you get some, Prue," commanded Tilly, diving into the mess.

Prue set aside her onion-chopping and trotted away in haste to the dark attic. But with a nose that smelled only onions, she got catnip and wormwood instead. Eager to be of use, she pounded up the herbs and scattered them into the large bowl.

"It doesn't smell just right, but I suppose it will when it is cooked, " said Tilly as she filled the empty turkey. Then, well satisfied with her work, she set it by till its hour came.

It took a long time to get the vegetables ready, for the girls thought they would have every sort. Eph helped, and by noon all was ready for cooking.

"Now you all go and sled while Prue and I set the table and get out the best china," said Tilly, bent on having her dinner look good, no matter what its other failings might be.

Out came the rough sleds, on went the round hoods, old hats, red cloaks, and moccasins, and away trudged the four younger Bassetts to amuse themselves in the snow.

Eph took his fiddle and scraped away in the parlor, while the girls, after a short rest, set the table. The cloth was coarse, but white as snow. They had no napkins and little silver; but the best tankard and Ma's few wedding spoons were set forth in state. The place of honor was left in the middle for the oranges yet to come.

"Doesn't it look beautiful?" said Prue when they paused.

"Pretty nice. I wish Ma could see it," began Tilly, when a loud howling startled both girls and sent them flying to the window.

The short afternoon had passed so quickly that twilight had come, and now they saw four small, black figures tearing up the road to come bursting in, all screaming at once, "The bear, the bear! Eph, get the gun!"

Eph had gotten down his gun before the girls could calm the children enough to tell their story.

"Down in the holler, sleddin', we heard a growl," began Sol, with eyes as big as saucers.

"I saw him first, lookin' over the wall," roared Seth.

"Aw-f-ful big and sh-shaggy," quavered Roxy, clinging to Tilly. Rhody hid in Prue's skirts and piped out, "His great paws kept clawing at us, and I was so scared my legs would hardly go."

"We ran as fast as we could, and he came growling after us. He's awful hungry," added Sol, looking about for a safe retreat.

"Eph, don't let him eat us," cried both little girls, flying upstairs to hide under their mother's bed.

"No danger of that, you little geese. I'll shoot him as soon as he comes. Get out of the way now, boys," Eph said as he raised the window.

"There he is! Don't miss!" cried Seth, following Sol, who had climbed to the top of the cupboard.

Prue stationed herself by the hearth as if bent on dying at her post. But Tilly boldly stood at the open window, ready to lend a hand if the enemy proved too much for Eph.

"Get the ax, Tilly, and if I should miss, stand ready to keep him off while I load again," said Eph.

Tilly flew for the ax and was at her brother's side by the time the bear was near enough to be dangerous.

"Fire, Eph!" cried Tilly firmly.

"Wait till he rears again. I'll get a better shot," answered the boy. Prue covered her ears, and the small boys cheered from their dusty refuge up among the pumpkins.

Suddenly Tilly threw down the ax, flung open the door, and ran straight into the arms of the bear, who stood up straight to receive her. The growlings changed to a loud "Haw, haw!" that startled the children more than the report of a gun.

"It's Gad Hopkins tryin' to fool us!" cried Eph.

"Gad! How could you scare us so?" laughed Tilly.

Gad drew a dozen oranges from some deep pocket and fired them into the kitchen window with such good aim that Eph ducked, Prue screamed, and Sol and Seth came down much quicker than they went up.

"Well, I upset my sleigh, and the horse left me, so I tied on my buffalo skins to tote 'em easy and walked till I saw the children sleddin'. I just meant to give 'em a little scare, but when they ran, I kept up the joke to see how Eph would like company," roared Gad, haw-hawing again.

"You'd have had a warm welcome if I'd put a bullet in you, old chap," said Eph, coming out with the children.

"Come in and have dinner with us," cried Tilly, trying to escape. "Pa will be along soon, I reckon."

"I can't. My folks will think I'm dead if I don't get along home," said Gad, taking a kiss from Tilly's rosy cheek. His own cheek tingled with the smart slap she gave him as she ran away, yelling that she hated bears and might use the ax next time.

"Sakes alive—the turkey is burnt on one side!" scolded Tilly.

"Well, I couldn't think of dinner when I expected to be eaten alive," said Prue, who had tumbled into the cradle when the rain of oranges began.

Tilly laughed and all the rest joined in. The spirits of the younger ones were revived with sucks from one orange which passed quickly from hand to hand. The older girls dished up the dinner and were struggling to get the pudding out of the cloth when Roxy called out, "Here's Pa!"

"There's folks with him," added Rhody.

"Lots of 'em! I see two big sleighs chock-full," shouted Seth.

"It looks like a funeral. Guess Gran'ma's dead and come up to be buried here," said Sol solemnly, causing the older children to run to the window to see.

"If that's a funeral, the mourners are uncommon jolly," said Eph, as merry voices and laughter broke the white silence without.

"I see fat Aunt Cinthy, and Cousin Hetty—and there's Moses

and Amos. I do declare, Pa's bringin' 'em all home to have some fun here," cried Prue.

"Oh, I'm so glad I got dinner!" cried Tilly, while the twins pranced and the small boys cheered.

The cheer was answered heartily as in poured Father, Mother, Baby, aunts, and cousins.

"Isn't Gran'ma dead at all?" asked Sol, in the midst of the kissing and hand-shaking.

"Bless your heart, no!" answered Ma. "It was all a mistake. Mother was sittin' up as chirk as you please, and dreadful sorry you didn't all come."

"What in the world set you to gettin' up such a supper?" asked Mr. Bassett, looking about him.

Tilly modestly began to tell, but the others broke in and sang her praises in a sort of chorus, in which bears, pies, and oranges were oddly mixed. Satisfaction was expressed by all, and Tilly and Prue served dinner, sure everything was perfect.

But when big Cousin Moses took the first taste of the stuffing, he nearly choked on the bitter morsel.

"Tilly Bassett, whatever made you put wormwood and catnip in your stuffin'?" demanded Ma, trying not to be severe, for all the rest were laughing and Tilly looked ready to cry.

"I did it," said Prue, nobly taking all the blame, which caused Pa to kiss her on the spot and declare that it didn't do a mite of harm, for the turkey was all right.

"Well, I've never seen onions cooked better," said Aunt Cinthy. "All the vegetables are well done, and the dinner is a credit to you, my dears."

The pudding was an utter failure, in spite of the blazing brandy in which it lay—as hard and heavy as one of the stone balls on a great gate. It was speedily whisked out of sight, and all fell upon the pies, which were perfect. But Tilly and Prue were depressed and didn't recover till the dinner was over and the evening fun was well under way.

"Blindman's buff," "hunt the slipper," and other lively games soon set everyone bubbling over with merriment. And when Eph struck up his fiddle, old and young fell into their places for a dance.

Apples and cider, chat, and singing finished the evening, and after a grand kissing all around, the guests drove off in the clear moonlight, which came just in time to cheer their long drive.

When the jingle of the last bell had died away, Mr. Bassett said soberly as they stood together on the hearth: "Children, we have special cause to be thankful that the sorrow we expected was changed into joy. So we'll read a chapter 'fore we go to bed and give thanks where thanks is due."

Then Tilly set out the light stand with the big Bible on it and a candle on each side, and all sat quietly in the firelight, smiling as they listened with happy hearts to the sweet old words that fit all times and seasons so beautifully.

When the "good nights" were over and the children in bed, Prue put her arm around Tilly, for she felt her older sister shaking and was sure she was crying.

"Don't mind about the old stuffin' and puddin', deary," Prue whispered tenderly, "because nobody cared. Ma said we really did do surprisin' well for such young girls."

The laughter Tilly was trying to smother broke out then and was so infectious that Prue could not help joining her, even before she knew the cause of the merriment.

"I was mad about the mistakes but don't care enough to cry. I'm laughing to think how Gad fooled Eph and I found him out. I thought Moses and Amos would have died over it when I told them, it was so funny," explained Tilly when she got her breath.

"I was so scared that when the first orange hit me, I thought it was a bullet and scrabbled into the cradle as fast as I could. It was real mean to frighten the little ones so," laughed Prue, as Tilly gave a growl.

Here a smart rap on the wall of the next room caused a sudden lull in the fun, and Mrs. Bassett's voice was heard, saying, "Girls, go to sleep immediate, or you'll wake the baby."

"Yes'm," answered two meek voices, and after a few irrepressible giggles, silence reigned, broken only by an occasional snore from the boys or the soft scurry of mice in the buttery, taking their part in this old-fashioned Thanksgiving.